CW00867200

Sleeping Beauty

Design: David Houghton
Printed in Hong Kong

Published by: Sanctuary Publishing Limited, The
Colonnades, 82 Bishops Bridge Road, London W2 6BB

CD Produced & Narrated by The Dreamteam

Featuring music from the symphony by Tchaikovsky used
with kind permission of KPM Music Limited

ISBN: 1-86074-178-9

Long ago in a faraway land of soft rolling hills and valleys lay a dark, unfriendly forest of cruel, tangled thorns. And in the midst of the thick forest stood an ancient, crumbling palace that no one ever visited.

One day a young Prince came riding by. He was a stranger from a distant kingdom and, seeing the tangled forest, he stopped to wonder how anyone could reach the palace within.

Suddenly a voice from behind made him jump. An old woman had appeared as if from nowhere.

"Young Prince," she said, for she could see he was of noble birth. "You are wondering what is in the old palace surrounded by these thorny woods, are you not?" The Prince admitted that he was. "Would you like me to tell you about it?" The Prince nodded. So the old woman began to tell the story of Sleeping Beauty.

This was once a happy place. After many childless years the King and Queen had a beautiful baby daughter whom they named Aurora and the entire land celebrated the joyous event.

The highest to the humblest brought gifts for the little Princess and among the presents were seven special gifts bestowed by seven Good Fairies.

The first Good Fairy bestowed the gift of beauty. The second, the gift of song. The third, the gift of happiness. The fourth, the gift of laughter. The fifth, the gift of kindness. The sixth, the gift of curiosity.

But before the seventh Good Fairy could bestow her gift something terrible happened. To everyone's horror the Wicked Fairy made her entrance.

"Good day to you, your Majesties, and thank you for your kind invitation."
"But we didn't invite you," began the King.
"Exactly!" screamed the Wicked Fairy. "But you all seem to be having a wonderful time without me! And my, what a beautiful baby!" she sneered. "And what wonderful gifts she has. What a happy life she would have had . . . "

"What do you mean?" cried the King in alarm.

"I mean," cackled the Wicked Fairy, "that it is time for me to bestow my gift on the little one."

"My gift to you, Princess Aurora," said the Wicked Fairy, turning to the baby, "my gift to you, sweet little Princess... shall be a curse!"

"Before you reach the age of sixteen, my dear, you will prick your finger on the spindle of a spinning wheel and die." And with that the Wicked Fairy disappeared in a whiff of smoke.

"Oh what can we do?" wailed the Queen. "Who can rid my baby of this terrible curse?"

The seventh Fairy, who had not yet bestowed her gift on Princess Aurora, flew down. The King asked her if she could reverse the curse.

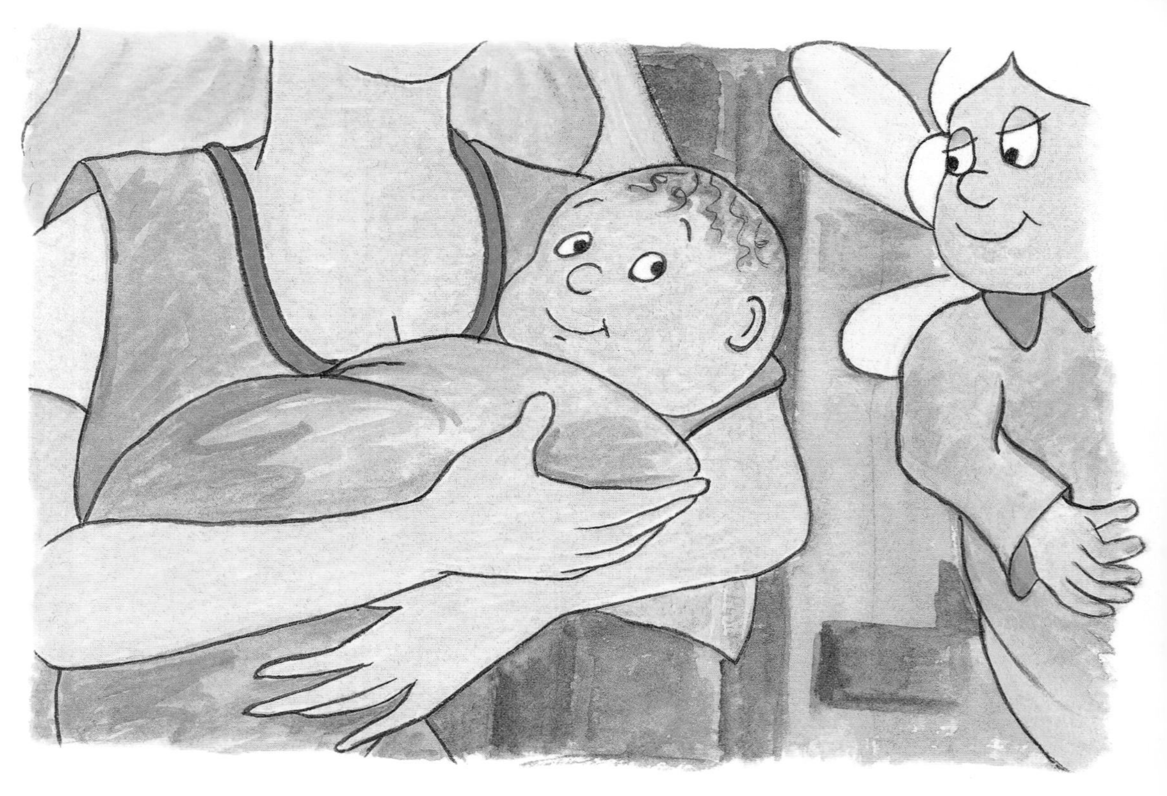

"Alas no," she replied. "The Wicked Fairy's magic is much too powerful. But this I can do . . . " and she turned to the Princess. "If you should prick your finger, fair Princess Aurora, you will not die, but will instead sleep for one hundred years unless you are awakened by the kiss of your true love."

The thought of their beautiful baby daughter sleeping for one hundred years was more than the King and Queen could bear. So, the King ordered by royal decree that every spinning wheel in the land be burned.

Without spinning wheels, there was no new cloth and without cloth the people of the kingdom had no new clothes.

But the years passed quickly and thanks to the gifts of the Good Fairies, the Princess grew into a beautiful and happy young woman. She too wore old and patched clothes, as did her parents, the King and Queen.

Soon the eve of Aurora's sixteenth birthday arrived.
"Nothing bad has happened so far," thought the King as he wandered through the palace. "What could possibly happen to her now? From tomorrow everything will be back to normal again."

But one of the Princess's gifts was curiosity. And another was kindness.
It was curiosity that took her into an unfamiliar
part of the palace that same day.

All around were beautiful new dresses the like of which the Princess had never seen before.

And sitting in the corner of the room was an old woman, bent over a spinning wheel.

"What are you doing?" asked Princess Aurora.
"I am spinning on my spinning wheel," said the old woman. "This is the only one in the kingdom, so I have to spin all the royal cloth myself . . . and I am old . . . and tired."

"I will help you," said Princess Aurora.
"But you don't know how to spin," said the old woman.
"I can learn," said the Princess. "You can teach me."
"Of course," said the old woman. "It's simple."

But as soon as Aurora sat at the spinning wheel, her hand touched the needle and she pricked her finger.

The Princess fell to the floor. Cackling, the Wicked Fairy disappeared without trace.

Elsewhere in the palace the King thought he had heard an unfamiliar sound. He paused for a moment trying to recall what it was. Of course! A spinning wheel.

Fearful for his daughter, he called the guards and set off to search the palace.

But it was too late. They found Princess Aurora on the floor. The spell had worked and she had fallen into a deep sleep.

The King and Queen were beside themselves with sorrow. The only thing the Good Fairy could do to ease their sadness, and to make sure the Princess would not be alone when she awoke, was to send the King and Queen to sleep for one hundred years too.

In fact, she sent everyone to sleep . . .

Now this angered the Wicked Fairy who, try as she might, could not reverse the Good Fairy's spell and wake up the sleeping people. If she couldn't reverse the sleeping spell, she would make sure no one would ever get near to the palace to rescue the Princess.

So she cast a spell to create a forest of the thickest thorns, each branch of which would grow back as soon as it was cut, fighting off anyone who tried to get through.

"This thorn forest grew and has guarded the palace ever since. And that is the story of the Sleeping Beauty . . ." said the old woman, as she finished her tale.

The Prince, who had listened carefully to the old woman's tale, asked, "Did Aurora have long, golden hair?"

"Yes," said the old woman.

"And deep blue eyes? And rose red lips?"

"Yes," she answered again, "but how do you know?"

"I have often dreamed about her," said the Prince, "and this tangled forest. That's why I stopped to investigate."

"Then you shall be the one to rescue the Princess." And with that the old woman transformed into the Good Fairy.

Hacking his way through the forest, the Prince set off to rescue the Princess. But true to the spell, as fast as he cut down the thorns, they grew again, thicker and stronger.

Seeing the Prince in trouble the Good Fairy decided to help and gave him a magical sword. It chopped through the thorns with ease and the Prince finally reached the palace steps.

He finally came to the room where Princess Aurora was sleeping. There the Wicked Fairy hovered at the foot of the steps which led up to the Princess's bed. But as with most wickedness, she had no power over true love and the Prince pushed her aside.

Reaching the Princess's bedside at last, the Prince kissed her on the lips.

Aurora awoke to see the Prince and instantly fell in love with him.

And as soon as the Princess was awake, the Good Fairy woke everybody else in the palace, greeting them with the triumphant news that a Prince had rescued the Princess.

The Prince and Princess were married soon after.

Happiness reigned throughout the kingdom and with their spinning wheels returned, the people could once again start spinning cloth for new clothes.

With her magic defeated, the Wicked Fairy left the kingdom, disappearing in a whiff of smoke, never to be seen there again.

also available in the series...

Swan Lake

ISBN: 1-86074-179-7
Price: £9.99

The time has come for Prince Siegfried to choose a bride. But the prince is not ready to marry and, seeking refuge in a summer house on the island in the middle of Swan Lake, he falls asleep, waking in darkness to see a flock of white swans whose reflections are not those of swans at all... Meanwhile the evil magician Rothbart, is working his spell to ensure that his beautiful daughter Odille, the black swan, is the bride.

Peter and the wolf

ISBN: 1-86074-177-0
Price: £9.99

A baby is rescued one snowy night by a wolf, who lays the child at the steps of a woodcutter's cottage. Many years later the same wolf, overcome by hunger, returns to the village. Will Peter remember the beast's kindness in time to rescue him from the three brave hunters' gunshot?

Toy Symphony

ISBN: 1-86074-180-0
Price: £9.99

Lucy's Nightingale has lost her magical song. Only Jack Frost can prepare the potion to restore it and the toys must help him gather the ingredients, So, Drum Major sets off to collect a wisp of thunder, Trumpet prepares to catch an arrow of hail, Triangle searches for the purest of notes, the Rattles must steal the whistle from the North wind and Quail flies off to collect the murmur of the White River. But can they succeed in time, before midnight on Christmas Eve?

Nutcracker

ISBN: 1-86074-181-9
Price: £9.99

When Uncle Drosselmier arrives at Marie and Fritz's house on Christmas Eve the children are in great expectation of the presents he will have brought. This year, his gift is very unusual – a nutcracker – of no particular significance to anyone but the Mouseking, who is watching from a distance...

also available...

Fiddley's First Friend

Our story begins a couple of months before Christmas in Santa Claus' workshop, where all the Gnomes are working hard, making toys to meet the Christmas rush. One Gnome decides to make a new type of toy and searching through Santa's archives for inspiration comes across a picture in an ancient book of a very strange looking creature called the Fiddley Foodle Bird. He proceeds to make a toy in its likeness.

Santa is unimpressed by the toy, that is until it comes to life and seems to possess the unique ability to grow, shrink and change colour according to whether anybody believes in him or not.

Accompanying CD includes 10 original songs and narration.

Price: £9.99

ISBN: 1-86074-178-9